To baby Scout,
welcome to the world.

First published in Great Britain in 2012 by Andersen Press Ltd.,
20 Vauxhall Bridge Road, London SW1V 2SA.
Published in Australia by Random House Australia Pty.,
Level 3, 100 Pacific Highway, North Sydney, NSW 2060.
Text and illustrations copyright © Michael Foreman, 2012.
The rights of Michael Foreman to be identified as the
author and illustrator of this work have been asserted by him
in accordance with the Copyright, Designs and Patents Act, 1988.
All rights reserved.
Colour separated in Switzerland by Photolitho AG, Zürich.
Printed and bound in Malaysia by Tien Wah Press.
Michael Foreman has used watercolours in this book.

10   9   8   7   6   5   4   3   2   1

British Library Cataloguing in Publication Data available.

ISBN 978 1 84939 451 2 (hardback)
ISBN 978 1 84939 519 9 (paperback)

This book has been printed on acid-free paper

NEWSPAPER BOY
AND
ORIGAMI GIRL!

MICHAEL FOREMAN

ANDERSEN PRESS

Every day, Joey, the newspaper boy, stood on the street corner trying to sell his newspapers and magazines.

People pushed, rushed and elbowed past him. He was often cold and hungry. At night he slept on the newspapers he hadn't managed to sell.

Late one cold autumn afternoon, a pack of young bullies grabbed Joey and stole what little money he had.

Suddenly, to Joey's surprise, his newspaper bag flew
into the air and the newspapers transformed into . . .

. . . *ORIGAMI GIRL!*

She leaped in amongst the bullies
and chased them off down the street,
but they disappeared into the dark
alleyways of the city . . .

"Oh no!" Joey cried. "They've got my money! And who are you anyway?"

"I'm Origami Girl," she said. "Don't worry, we'll find them and get your money back."

She quickly folded a pair of wings out of newspaper.

"Climb up onto my back," she said.

Origami Girl spread her wings and they soared up high above the city. From here they could look down into the alleyways . . .

. . . and soon spotted the group of bullies as they ran through the streets, snatching first an old lady's bag and then a little boy's mobile phone.

The bullies joined up with other gangs and they all headed into an old tumble-down building by the river.

Origami Girl and Joey landed on the roof. The room below was crowded with bullies, burglars, robbers and rascals of all kinds. In the middle, a fat old man sat counting money and examining jewels through a big magnifying glass.

Origami Girl crashed through the skylight onto the table and dived in amongst the crooks, somersaulting, spinning, back-flipping, cartwheeling and knocking them over like skittles.

Meanwhile, Joey spotted the
fat crook creeping out of
the back door and down the
steps to the river.

He parachuted down, 'bagged' him with his newspaper bag . . .

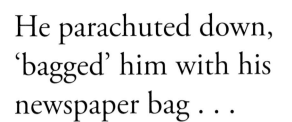

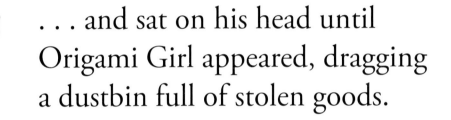

. . . and sat on his head until Origami Girl appeared, dragging a dustbin full of stolen goods.

She stuffed the fat crook into the dustbin and then ripped a huge poster off a theatre wall.

Quickly, she folded it into the body of a beautiful origami swan . . .

. . . and transformed herself into the neck and head.

Together they sailed with the fat crook and the dustbin, down the river to the River Police.

The fat crook was arrested and people came to reclaim their stolen goods.

During the excitement no one, apart from Joey, noticed the origami swan unfold back into a bundle of newspapers and slip into Joey's newspaper bag.

The next day Joey's picture was on the front page of all the newspapers above the headline:

"THE BOY WHO BAGGED THE BIG BAD BOSS!"

And as for Origami Girl she was happy to be snug, back in Joey's newspaper bag . . . waiting for the next adventure.